I'm serious—I don't mind depositing all this money. Go home and sleep!
Thanks, Bob! See you tomorrow, then.
24 Hour Store

BOOF

We're rich!
Let's get away with this first!

Where's the van?
I thought I parked it here.

We need to get outta here quick!

You shouldn't have left the keys in the van.

Fish sticks?

LUNCH
Jarrett J. Krosoczka

LADY
and the Summer Camp Shakedown
Fish Stick Nunchucks
Alfred A. Knopf New York

Two weeks of summer camp, here we come!
CAMP

Ohhhhhhh boy . . . pinch me.

Oh, come on, it's not that bad.

I mean, sure—they don't let us bring video games.

Or computers. Or any electronics for that matter.

Oh man. This is going to stink!

Guys, we've been looking forward to sleepaway camp since we were kids! We're finally old enough.

Don't worry, losers–if I don't make this a miserable experience for you, then the swamp monster will!
So true, Milmoe.
15

Oh please, there's no swamp monster.
But there is!

And I hear he eats up any kid who loses at the Cabin Wars. So, Hector, you're out of luck!
Ha!

HA! HA! HAW!
Save it, Milmoe!

Meanwhile . . .

Smell that fresh air, Betty!

Mmm-hmm!

Our gadgets are packed away and it's worry-free from here on out! Perfect day to set up the mess hall for the first day of camp!

Bug juice, cookouts, s'mores . . . makes my heart flutter!
Nothing quite like camp!
CAMP
Here's to summer!
Just take every day as it comes!
Looks like Camp Director Jed has assembled a great group of counselors this year.

There's Scott, the returning lifeguard. He's always been the most popular.
I never knew what the girls saw in him.
Girls' counselor Hilary has always had a crush on him.
Who hasn't she had a crush on?
Alice had a thing for Scott, too.
Oh boy.
Nicole is the new boating instructor.
Whatever floats her boat, I guess.
There's Jeff. I'm not sure Jeff ever really knows what's going on.
Or where he is, even!
Then there's the new counselor— Ben. He's a looker!
I'll say! Stops my blender in seconds flat!

Looks like some of the girls' counselors have already taken notice.
There's Assistant Camp Director Ray Magee. He's been the assistant for so many years. I thought for sure that he would be promoted to camp director.
But it looks like they passed him up for Adam Jed, last year's new guy.
Attention, staff!
I wonder if he's bitter.
This is going to be a very exciting summer! We have a great group of campers on their way.
HONK! HONK!

It's the campers! They're here!

Welcome, campers!
Yeah!
Woo-hoo!
CAMP
MESS HALL
CAMP FUN TIMES

Yay, campers!

OMG, these are going to be the best two weeks ever!
In all of history? How is that even possible?

This is all so lame. . . .
Let me help you with your bags and stuff.

See you guys around, I guess.

What are you guys doing here?!

C'mon, campers! Let's go meet your bunkmates!
C'mon, this is totally going to be killer!
Good luck, Dee.

Good to see you guys!
I hope they don't cause any trouble.

At one of the boys' cabins . . .
Welcome home, dudes!
Who farted?
Whoever smelt it dealt it!
Wanna see something gross?
Milmoe, look! Those losers are in our cabin!
They'd better not drag us down in the Cabin Wars!

At one of the girls' cabins . . .
Did you see how cute the boys in Cabin 5 are?
Cabin, sweet cabin!
Let's all make friendship bracelets in Arts and Crafts!
Who would you say is the cutest counselor this year?
Ben, by far!

That night at the opening campfire . . .
We counselors are so excited that you're finally here!

But be warned of the terrible swamp monster!

Oh, come on, Scott! There's no need to scare them.

But they should know the story . . .

. . . of the evil swamp monster!

He lives at the bottom of the pond and eats squirrels for lunch!

He has legs the size of tree trunks!

And fangs as sharp as knives!

On the rare occasion a camper wanders off alone . . .

ARGGGGGHHHHH!!!

All right, all right, everyone, calm down. There is no swamp monster here at camp.

After the campfire, the campers are on their way back to their cabins. . . .
You don't think that the swamp monster exists, do you?
Scott did have a good story.
BWAAH!
HA! He exists and he'll eat you in your sleep!
HA! HA! HA!

OK, campers, lights out.

Hey, Terrence.
Terrence.

What,
Hector?

I'm scared.

Go to sleep!

Guys, quiet down, please. We've got a big day ahead of us tomorrow. . . .

Aaaaaaaaaaagh!

What happened?
Something came out of the woods and attacked me!

We heard the commotion! Are you OK, Ben?
It was huge! Hideous!
Ha, ha. Very funny, counselors. Everyone back to your bunks.
B-b-but . . . it was a real monster! It looked like it came from the pond or something!
It smashed up my guitar!
Back to your bunks.

Don't worry about this mess, we'll clean it up.
Thanks, Lunch Lady.

I was looking forward to relaxing afternoons in a canoe, but it looks like our vacation is ending before it begins!

And I even brought my flippers to swim with!

The sooner this mystery is solved, the sooner we can get back to our summer fun.

I'll bring samples of this slime back to my lab.

Baked beans! Look! Monster footprints. Or so they seem.
Lollipop Magnifying Glass
Cookie-Camera
click

The next day at lunch . . .
CAMP FUN TIMES
I hear he's ten feet tall!
I hear he has a thousand teeth!

I hear he can swallow a grown man in one gulp!
His pond scum is radioactive!
His stare can freeze you on the spot!

What?!

No fair!

The waterfront is the best part of camp!

We can't take any chances if something is out there.
Nicole, you will now be assigned pool duty with Scott.

This whole thing stinks! Ray Magee never liked waterfront activities!

C'mon, Ben! Are you really going to whine about being attacked by a mythical creature?

Don't listen to him.
Ben, are you OK?

Ben, can I get you anything?

Don't worry about it, Alice, I'll help Ben out. Ben, I got you a new guitar.
Do you think you can still play?
I could try.

What are you going to wear to the camp dance?
I don't know, I still haven't decided.

Hey, guys.
The Cabin Wars are going to be awesome!
My bunkmates are driving me nuts!
We'll so crush skulls!
We hear ya!

I say tonight we sneak out and raid the kitchen for ice cream sandwiches.
No way! Not with that maniac swamp monster roaming around camp!
FART FART FART
C'mon, you don't believe in that mumbo jumbo, do you? It's just something that the counselors are setting up to scare us campers. Besides, we're talking about ice cream sandwiches here!
Mmm. Ice cream sandwiches.

Meanwhile, in Lunch Lady's makeshift headquarters . . .
There's bacteria in this slime found on the scene of the alleged swamp monster attack. It matches the bacteria in the samples I took from the camp pond.
PAPER PLATES
MUSTARD
BATH TISSUE
PLASTIC CUTLERY SPORK SUPPLY
SOUP
BATH TISSUE
48 COUNT
PAPER TOWELS
24 COUNT
PAPER TOWELS
BATH TISSUES

And the footprints don't match those of any wildlife from this region.

Could we be dealing with a real monster here?
gulp

Unpack the gadgets, Betty. Tonight we're Salisbury-staking out the pond!

That night . . .
I'm freaking out!

Focus on the ice cream sandwiches, Hector!

We're toast if anyone catches us!
I scream, you scream, we all scream for ice cream. . . .

KITCHEN
Shhhh!
SQUEAK

CAMP FUN TIMES

ICE CREAM

Sorry to bother you!
Please, continue eating.
Yeah, we were just leaving.
gulp

CRASH!
CRASH!

Oh, oatmeal! I don't see a thing.
I don't hear a thing.
Taco-vision Night Goggles
Hamburger Headphones

Wait!
I hear something.

I hear pots and pans!
The mess hall! Let's go!

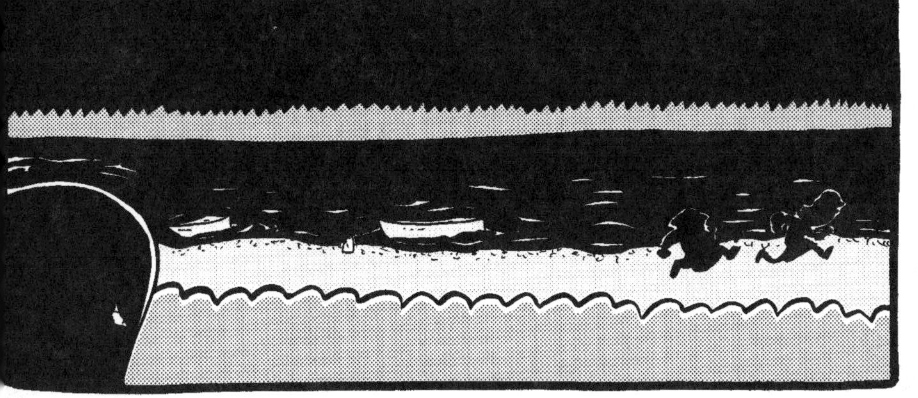

I think I just
peed my pants.

What in the chocolate
pudding is going on?
It wasn't us!
It was the
swamp
monster!

We sneaked out of our bunks, but look!
Slime!

He's right. Looks like pond slime.

Nobody messes with the mess hall! This monster will *pay*!

Kids, back to your bunks. Betty and I have some cleaning up to do. In more ways than one!

At Arts and Crafts the next morning . . .
Become one with your clay pots!
This swamp monster doesn't know who he's messing with.
Knead the clay, love the clay!
What do you suppose he wants with Lunch Lady?
Is he onto her?

Hey, are you guys talking about Lunch Lady?
Maybe, why?
She makes the best grilled cheese sandwiches. I just love her.
Yeah, well, she's the lunch lady at our school. So we kind of, like, know her.
OK, campers, time to wrap things up and head to lunch.
You guys are SO lucky!
Well, I need to get ready for the guitar lesson that I'm teaching this afternoon. You guys should sign up! See ya around.

So are we all still signing up for woodworking this afternoon?
A+C

Well, I've always wanted to learn how to play the guitar.
So I was thinking of maybe signing up for Ben's guitar lesson. Have a good lunch, guys.

Dee and guitar lessons?
That's odd.

At lunch . . .
Attention, all campers and staff! Ray Magee has notified me that he found slime on our premises. We think the swamp monster, or whatever this mysterious creature may be, attacked this very mess hall last night.
FUN
TIMES

I didn't tell him, did you?

No.

We will have no other choice but to cancel all evening activities.
What about the dance?!
Canceled.
We will also be canceling all outdoor activities.
What about the Cabin Wars?
Too dangerous.
Furthermore, we are canceling all afternoon sign-ups while we investigate.
Just when you think camp can't get any less fun!
This is so lame!
I can't believe this!

It's mass hysteria out there!

Guys, we need to put a stop to this!
We're going to expose the swamp monster for what he is—an elaborate prank!
What are we going to do about it?!
Um . . . that was a legitimate monster we saw last night!

Oh man! I was so looking forward to the camp dance!
I know. I was going to ask Ben for a dance.
I was going to ask Ben for a dance!
This swamp monster is out of line! I'm going to hunt down the monster myself!

That sounds dangerous! Aren't you scared?
I'm not afraid of anything.
I'll see you ladies after I've defeated the monster and brought peace back to camp!

He's so brave!
Well, you can have Ben. I was going to ask Scott to dance anyhow.
No way, Scott is mine!

Let's check to see if the Milk-Cam picked up any footage of the swamp monster's mess hall mayhem.
Lunch Tray Laptop
clickity-clack
MILK-CAM

Whatever it is, it took out our cameras!

I've finished my latest gadgets. I think they will help us put an end to this swamp monster.

Bacon and eggs! What are they?!
They're an Underwater Bendy-Straw Breathing Apparatus and an Underwater Mixer-Propulsion Backpack.

If I could only find some clues.
Nothing!

CRACK—

Who's that?

Scott the lifeguard?

RRRRRRR.....

Going for a swim, Lunch Lady? I thought we made it very clear that waterfront activities were off-limits!
RRR RRRRRRRRRRRRRRRRRRRRRRRR

Um . . . I, ah . . . was looking for fish. Yeah, fish to cook for lunch tomorrow.

See? Nothing like fresh fish! Only the best for our campers!
Well, get back to shore, where it's safe. I'll be sure to put this indiscretion in your file.
RRRRRRRRRR

I bet you anything that Assistant Camp Director Magee has been staging all of this swamp monster business.

Well, he does seem to enjoy canceling all of the activities. Maybe he's using the swamp monster thing as an excuse to squash all the camp fun!
C'mon. Let's follow him!
Do we have to?
You could stay here and hope the swamp monster turns up.
Wait up, I'm comin'!

Lunch Lady! Come in, Lunch Lady!

Hey, Betty.
Spork Phone

I took another look at the slime from Ben's attack under the microscope.
Mole Communicator

I found traces of chlorine.

What would a swamp monster be doing hanging out by the pool?

Working on his tan?

I'll go check it out.

I'll meet you there.

A+C

I didn't realize that Ray Magee was artsy.
But he could be *crafty* enough to be making a swamp monster costume.
I knew it!
RAY MAGEE, WE KNOW WHAT YOU'RE UP TO!

You're making a . . . banner welcoming the new camp director.
And what are you doing out of your bunks?
Guys, let's get out of here! If the swamp monster isn't Ray, Lunch Lady might have a real beast on her hands! She's going to need our help!
CONGRATULATIONS
TO THE NEW CAMP DIRECTOR!

At the pool . . .
Come out, come out, wherever you are!
Hmmm . . . the storage shed.
Let's see what's behind door number one.

CRASH!

ROOOAAR!!!

SPLOOSH!

CRASH!

Did you find anything?

He's headed toward the pond! We can't let him get away.
S'more Star
It's time for a cookout!

Let's BBQ!
Hot Sauce Laser

You kids get back here! You should be in your bunks!
I don't know what's scarier—a swamp monster or an angry Ray Magee!
C'mon, we can outrun this guy!
Let's grab Milmoe's Cabin Wars supplies. He hides them under our cabin!

Shortly after . . .
Water balloons filled with mud . . . water guns filled with rotten eggs . . .
This is the one time I'm glad Milmoe plays dirty!
Let's go!

THERE HE IS!
THWUCK

BZZZZZZZZZZZZZ
ZZZZZZZ
CRACK

CRASH!
HOLD IT RIGHT THERE, SCUM MONSTER!

GET HIM!!!
SPLAT! SQUISH! SPLAT!
HIIYAH!

POW!
He's escaping to the pond!
Wish me luck!

He's a fast swimmer!
But he's no match for the Underwater Mixer-Propulsion Backpack!

I wonder how many fish tacos we could make out of this guy.

It looks like a rubber mask!
Well then, let's see who's under there!

LIFEGUARD SCOTT!

Just as I suspected! What's the matter, Casanova, you can't handle playing second fiddle to the new guy?

I'm supposed to be the number one counselor at camp. Everyone loved my stories, and all of the girls' counselors wanted to dance with me—until Ben showed up! I thought if I could scare people a little, make Ben look like a wimp, I would be on top again.

Pack your bags, Scott. You are fired!
Justice is served!

And what are the two of you doing by the pond anyhow? Didn't I ask you to stay away?
Like I said, I was fishing.
Yeah, that's when the "monster" jumped out and attacked us!
Lucky for us, these campers saved us.
They may have saved you, but they were running around camp unsupervised. These indiscretions will be reported in their files!

The next night . . .
What's the point of dancing anyhow?
Oh, Dee.
MESS HALL
CAMP FUN TIMES

I'm a-gonna make it funky, yee-ow!
MARK THE SHARK

Guys, could this get any worse? They're playing Evan McFunky music! Blech!
Look at that girl, shakin' those hips. I just want to kiss her lips! Yee-ow!
Hey, Dee.

Hey, guys. Cool music, huh?
Oh, hi, Ben. Yeah.

Hey, look! There are my dates for the evening!

She's gonna be kissin' me! One-two-three-yeah-eh-eh! Ow, ow,
Hey, Ben! Let's get our groovy grooves on!

C'mon, kids, get hip with it.
Shake what ya momma gave ya, Betty!
Oh yeah, it's my birthday!

FOR ALL OF MY FRIENDS FROM THE HOLE IN THE WALL GANG CAMP.
—J.J.K.

THIS IS A BORZOI BOOK PUBLISHED BY ALFRED A. KNOPF

Visit us on the Web! www.randomhouse.com/kids

Educators and librarians, for a variety of teaching tools,
visit us at www.randomhouse.com/teachers

Library of Congress Cataloging-in-Publication Data
Krosoczka, Jarrett J.
Lunch Lady and the summer camp shakedown / Jarrett J. Krosoczka. — 1st ed.
p. cm.
Summary: When the crime-fighting school lunch lady works as the cook at summer camp, she investigates the mystery of the legendary swamp monster.
ISBN 978-0-375-86095-9 (trade pbk.) — ISBN 978-0-375-96095-6 (lib. bdg.)
1. Graphic novels. [1. Graphic novels. 2. Camps—Fiction. 3. Mystery and detective stories.] I. Title.
PZ7.7.K76Lus 2010
741.5'973—dc22
2009039783

The text of this book is set in Hedge Backwards.
The illustrations in this book were created using ink on paper and digital coloring.

MANUFACTURED IN MALAYSIA
May 2010
10 9 8 7 6 5 4 3 2 1

First Edition